There he is.
Just look at him.

I could topple him with a tap!

YEAH!

No way am I standing in *that* line.

Mmmmmmm...at least his lunch is good.

Better than mine.

Bet his home is better than mine too.

Older brothers, y'know...

Next day at school, I shove him extra hard.
Just cuz I can.

Someone sees me do it.

TATTLETALE

I end up in the office.

The principal tells me to try.
My potential...

BLAH
BLAH
BLAH
BLAH
BLAH
BLAH
BLAH
BLAH
BLAH

I look down like I feel bad.
Mostly I just feel mad.

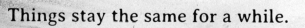

Things stay the same for a while.

Until...

Huh. Skinny Kid's having a party.
Everyone's invited.

ARE YOU GOING?

SURE, WHY NOT?

Even me.

I LOVE PARTIES!

WHATEVER...

I'm so *not* going.

The morning of, I look out my window.

I let the sun warm me up for a while.

I put on my best shirt

and go.

When I get there,
everyone's holding a gift.

I put my hands in my pockets.

I walk down the pathway

up the stairs

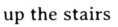

to the front door.

I see Skinny Kid's mom inside,
holding his birthday cake.

Everyone is celebrating in the kitchen.

I stay in the living room.

huh...

Forever in our hearts

Love you. Dad

I slump down in a chair,
kicking air.

I hear a sound and look up.

His mom is in the doorway,
like she knows I'm there.

She sees me...

Like **SEES** me.

She marches

right up

to me.

She says in a real quiet voice . . .

"Jimmy, what would you like for lunch tomorrow?"

"I hear you like my lunches."

"Here's what I'm gonna do. I'm going to make a *second* lunch.
And my son will bring it for you, every day."

"Okay?"

And do you know something?

She did!

And *that's* how I got lunch every day. . .

and a whole lot more.

Cataloging-in-Publication Data (by Cassidy Cataloging)

Otoshi, Kathryn
Lunch every day / by Kathryn Otoshi.

1st edition. Temecula, CA: KO Kids Books, ©2021
Audience: Ages 4 and up.
Summary: Based on a true story of a boy named Jimmy who
takes another kid's lunch at school every day. But through the
power of kindness, he is transformed into a compassionate
human being. --Publisher.
ISBN: 9781734348200
LCSH: Bullies--Juvenile fiction. | Bullying--Juvenile fiction.
| Victims of bullying--Juvenile fiction. | Interpersonal conflict
in children--Juvenile fiction. | School children--Food--Juvenile
fiction. | Courage--Juvenile fiction. | Kindness--Juvenile fiction.
| Compassion--Juvenile fiction. | CYAC: Bullies--Fiction. |
Bullying--Fiction. | Interpersonal conflict--Fiction. | School
children--Food--Fiction. | Courage--Fiction. | Kindness--
Fiction. | Compassion--Fiction.

LCC: PZ7.O8775 L86 2021 | DDC: [Fic]--dc22

KO KIDS BOOKS
31768 Loma Linda Rd.
Temecula, CA 92592

Distributed by Publishers Group West/Ingram
www.pgw.com (866) 400-5351

Printed in China

AUTHOR'S NOTE

Jim Perez has been an educator in Southern California for over 20 years. Under his leadership, he and his innovative team have helped hundreds of thousands of kids through their bullying prevention programs, gang interventions, and community building leadership services.

This book is dedicated to Jim – one of the most remarkable human beings I've ever met.

And to the lady who kept making all those lunches for him, day after day.

K.O.